The Magic School Bus

BLOWS ITS TOP

A BOOK ABOUT VOLCANOES

SCHOLASTIC INC.
New York   Toronto   London   Auckland   Sydney
Mexico City   New Delhi   Hong Kong   Buenos Aires

From an episode of the animated TV series
produced by Scholastic Entertainment Inc.
Based on *The Magic School Bus* books
written by Joanna Cole and illustrated by Bruce Degen.

TV tie-in adaptation by Gail Herman and illustrated by Bob Ostrom.
TV script written by Brian Meehl and Jocelyn Stevenson.

ISBN 0-590-50835-0

55 54 53 52 51 50 49   40   14/0

Printed in the U.S.A.

It started like any ordinary day in Ms. Frizzle's class. But that doesn't mean much — there *aren't* any ordinary days in Ms. Frizzle's class.

That morning we were trying to put together an enormous globe. But we didn't have all the pieces, so the whole thing fell apart.

"Carlos," said Dorothy Ann, her nose in the instruction book, "if you spent more time on research, you would know how to put this globe together!"

Carlos dusted himself off. "And if you didn't spend so much time doing research, you could have helped!" he answered.

Ms. Frizzle looked over the mess. "I'm afraid you can't put that globe together until you have all the pieces," she told us. "You see, there's an island so new, it hasn't been discovered yet!"

"How can there be a *new* island?" asked Phoebe. "The earth never changes. Does it?"

"The earth is changing all the time," said Ms. Frizzle. "Right under your very feet."

We all looked down at our feet, but nothing was moving.

Dorothy Ann wanted to find clues to the island in her books. But Carlos wanted *us* to search for the mystery island. That way we could name it!

"What an explosive idea!" said Ms. Frizzle happily. "To the bus!"

Oh, no! Not another field trip!

"This is your captain speaking," announced Ms. Frizzle when we settled onboard. "On behalf of my flight crew, I want to thank you for flying the Magic School Bus."

We knew what that meant! Quickly we fastened our seat belts. Then we put our seats in an upright position.

Why does this always happen?

The Magic School Bus began to spin and stretch and pull. The next thing we knew, we were high in the air!

Soon we were flying over the ocean. The sky grew dark, and big black clouds floated past.

"The island should be arriving any minute now!" announced Ms. Frizzle.

How could an island just arrive? we wondered. But then thunder boomed and lightning streaked across the sky. The ocean beneath us bubbled like a pot of boiling water. From out of nowhere, a blanket of dark ash covered our windows.

"Prepare to land!" shouted Ms. Frizzle.

The bus grew surfboard pontoons, and we surfed to a stop right on top of the water. We all climbed off the bus. There was no land anywhere in sight. But Ms. Frizzle had an inflatable life raft. Carlos jumped in first. *Splash!* A big wave washed over the pontoon — sending Dorothy Ann's bookbag flying out to sea.

"I need my books to find that island!" wailed Dorothy Ann as the books sank. "We have to get them. Please, Ms. Frizzle. Please!"

Couldn't we just go to a bookstore?

"Of course we'll get them," agreed Ms. Frizzle. "Prepare to dive, class."

Everyone climbed back onto the bus. Then the Friz pressed a button and the Magic School Bus twisted into a submarine.

Carlos decided to stay on the raft. He wanted to be the first to spot the new island. Arnold stayed, too — but for another reason. He'd already had enough of our field trip.

We waved good-bye while Carlos, Arnold, and Liz buckled up their life jackets. "Batten down the hatches," the Friz called loudly, and down, down, down we went.

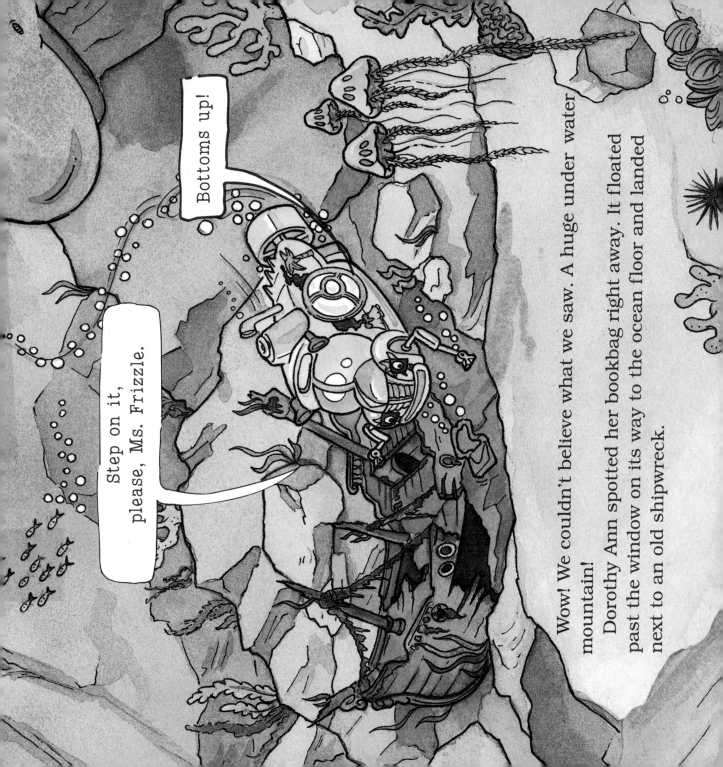

Bottoms up!

Step on it, please, Ms. Frizzle.

Wow! We couldn't believe what we saw. A huge under water mountain!

Dorothy Ann spotted her bookbag right away. It floated past the window on its way to the ocean floor and landed next to an old shipwreck.

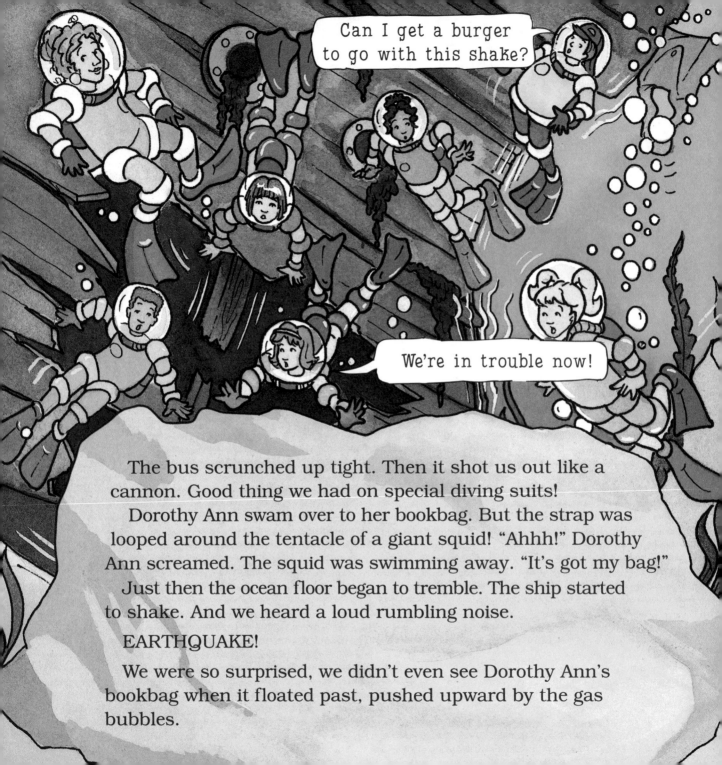

Can I get a burger to go with this shake?

We're in trouble now!

The bus scrunched up tight. Then it shot us out like a cannon. Good thing we had on special diving suits!

Dorothy Ann swam over to her bookbag. But the strap was looped around the tentacle of a giant squid! "Ahhh!" Dorothy Ann screamed. The squid was swimming away. "It's got my bag!"

Just then the ocean floor began to tremble. The ship started to shake. And we heard a loud rumbling noise.

EARTHQUAKE!

We were so surprised, we didn't even see Dorothy Ann's bookbag when it floated past, pushed upward by the gas bubbles.

"It says right here the earth's surface is made up of layered crustlike plates of rock that fit together like a jigsaw puzzle," he told Arnold. "These plates move very very slowly. But sometimes one plate slides under another one. When it slides, we can actually feel the earth move."

That's what the canyon was — two giant plates of rock. They were sliding together, creating an earthquake. And leave it to Ms. Frizzle to squeeze us right between them!

Carlos, you sound like Dorothy Ann!

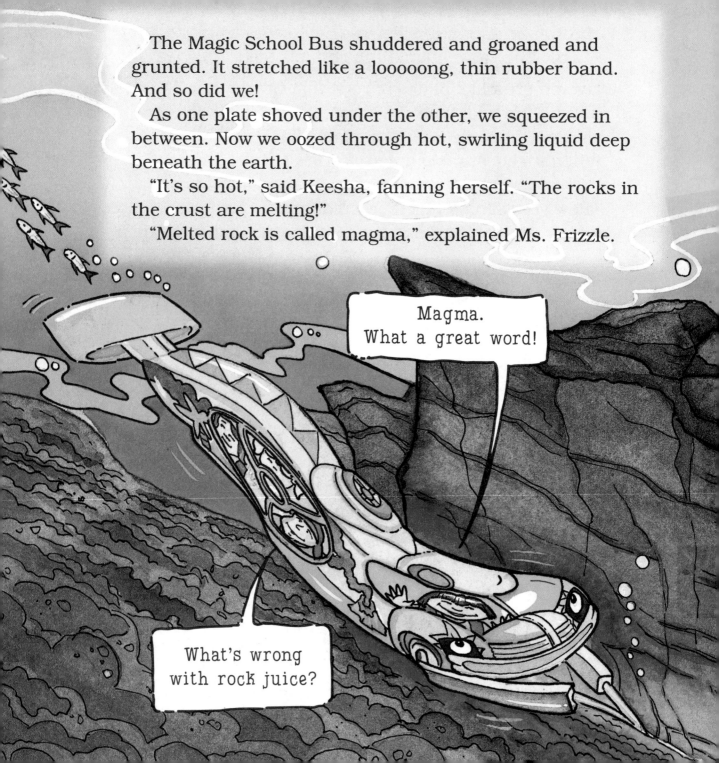

The Magic School Bus shuddered and groaned and grunted. It stretched like a looooong, thin rubber band. And so did we!

As one plate shoved under the other, we squeezed in between. Now we oozed through hot, swirling liquid deep beneath the earth.

"It's so hot," said Keesha, fanning herself. "The rocks in the crust are melting!"

"Melted rock is called magma," explained Ms. Frizzle.

Magma.
What a great word!

What's wrong
with rock juice?

Dorothy Ann wrinkled her nose. She was trying to figure it all out. She remembered the chimneys and the heat under the ocean floor, the earthquakes and the mountain. "We're under an underwater volcano!" she shouted.

Geysers shot up to the sky. Water hissed all around the raft. The rumbling noise grew louder, and Carlos waved his book excitedly. He'd figured out the very same thing!

Bingo, Dorothy Ann. And you figured it out by yourself.

According to my research, we're floating above a volcano!

Under the volcano, the magma pushed us up, up, up. Soon we were rising up in a big blob of boiling hot bubbles.

"Welcome to the magma chamber," said Ms. Frizzle grandly. "The heart of the volcano."

The pressure grew stronger and stronger. The magma rose higher.

Ralphie gulped. "How do we get out of here?" he asked.

"Out of a volcano?" Ms. Frizzle repeated. "How do you suppose?"

Dorothy Ann was too excited to be scared. "When all this magma shoots up and hits the air, it will cool down. Right?" she asked Ms. Frizzle.

"Absolutely," said Ms. Frizzle.

"And when it cools, it will harden into rock?"

"Eventually," Ms. Frizzle agreed.

"And the new rock will build up the top of this volcano," Dorothy Ann continued, "until it sticks out of the water. It will be a brand-new island!"

"Yessss!" shouted the Friz.

Just then we shot up through the bubbling magma like a rocket-ship. Higher . . . higher . . . closer to the top . . . *Clunk!* We jolted to a stop.

"Oh, no!" cried Dorothy Ann. "We've stopped rising."

"Something must be plugging up the volcano!" said Keesha.

"And the magma's squeezing us!" Phoebe exclaimed.

Carlos had no idea we were in such a tight spot. He still had his head buried in Dorothy Ann's books. "A lot of stuff is blown out of a volcano when it erupts," he told Arnold. "Volcanic ash and dust and rocks . . ."

Just then volcanic ash and dust and rocks rained down.

"And then lava," Carlos finished triumphantly. "Put it all together and you get — "

"Out of here!" Arnold exclaimed in a panic.

"No!" Carlos corrected. "You get Carlos Island!"

It will be a whole island named after ME!

Meanwhile, we'd jumped into our antimagma gear and were pushing the plug with all our might. But it wouldn't budge.

That's when Ms. Frizzle and the Magic School Bus went into action. They rammed the plug, again and again!

Kapow! The plug popped out. The magma boiled into glowing clouds of ash and rock. Then it all billowed out with a rush of steam.

What a sight! Red-hot lava poured down the sides of the volcano. The volcano grew bigger and bigger. . . .

It was an island!

Wheee! We landed — *plop!* — into the raft. Then the volcano belched one last time and the Magic School Bus whooshed into the air. A parachute opened, and the bus drifted down to a soft landing on the water.

"To Carlos Island!" said Carlos as we rowed over to the brand-new island. "I discovered it with the help of Dorothy Ann's books."

"Carlos Island? You mean Dorothy Ann Island," Dorothy Ann corrected. "*I* discovered it. And, for once, I didn't need my books."

But someone else had *landed* there first. Liz!

Ta-da!

So when Carlos and Dorothy Ann decided to write a book about their experiences, they knew exactly what to call it.

"*Lizard Island* by Carlos and Dorothy Ann!" said Carlos.

"Don't you mean *Lizard Island* by Dorothy Ann and Carlos?" said Dorothy Ann.

Dear Carlos,

My schoolbus never surfs, dives, stretches, or flies. And I can't believe yours does either!

Very truly yours,

Two Feet on the Ground

Dear Carlos,

I thought your book was a blast! But according to my research, it takes a lot longer than a few minutes for a volcano to grow from an undersea mountain into an island. Also, I don't think you should go wandering around inside a volcano, hang around one when it is erupting, or walk on lava right after the eruption. That would be too dangerous!

All my lava,

Ann E. Ruption

Dear Dorothy Ann,

Where did you buy your bookbag? You obviously have the latest in waterproof accessories!

Signed,

Your Shopping Friend

Memo to: Parents, Teachers, and Kids

This book describes how one underwater volcano can become an island. Sometimes two big pieces of the earth's crust — called plates — slide into one another, creating tremendous heat and pressure, melting the rock. The melted rock is magma. Over time, gases in the magma create pressure. Eventually that pressure blows the top off the volcano and the magma shoots out. As lava and dust and rocks flow out, they cover the volcano, layer by layer, until it breaks the ocean surface and makes an island! A volcano on land works the same as one in the sea. But there *are* different types of volcanoes. Some form where plates pull apart. Others form over hot spots in the crust.

P.S. There's never a fire in a volcano. There's only heat, so water can't put it out.

Ms. Frizzle